S0-CKU-048

"My eyes are blue, my hair is fair,
You'll see I have a big armchair,
It suits me well for all my trips,
And I can fly around in it.
I'm lovely, sweet, the smallest too,
So what's my name? I now ask you.
Try and guess it, if you can,
Yes! You've guessed! That's who I am!"

"Why glare at me as now you do?
I may seem like a hag to you,
And maybe too a witch, you fear,
But in the end all will be clear.
I dress in black from head to toe,
My parrot goes where e'er I go.
Be quick and say now who I am,
Don't make me angry, try again!"

"Ugly as my face may be,
Athlete there is none like me.
I dive right down with utmost glee,
To other worlds beneath the sea.
I have a leg of wood and nails,
(This may of course seem odd as snails).
Wasps pull me on my flight,
Guess my name and get it right!"
I conduct an orchestra with ease,
In teaching music I do please.
I play and sing quite decently
And often make up poetry.
My long black hair streams on high,
When on my chopping board I fly.
From the Orient I have come,
Guess now my name from this sum!"

"The last and shortest verse is mine,
So tired am I of this rhyme,
Of waiting for you all to guess
Who we are from how we dress.
As you can see, I'm in red and white,
So hurry up, I'm tired tonight!"

Hello,

We fairies need a vacation too, now and
then . . . so I'm sending my top fairies
(Iris, Tulip, Nettle, Orchid, Apricot
and Pine Cone) for a short stay in the
gnomes' village.

I hope they enjoy themselves and
keep out of mischief.

If anyone doesn't behave herself,
perhaps some young reader will
let me know . . .

With an enchanted kiss
from your own

Fairy Queen

Published in the United States of America by
Rand McNally & Company, 1984
© 1983 Piero Dami Editore, Italy
All rights reserved
Printed in Italy G.E.P. - Cremona

ISBN O-528-82564-X

Library of Congress Catalog Card No. 84-60931
Text adaptation
by Muriel Crawford

The Woodland Folk in
Fairyland

Tony Wolf

Rand McNally & Company

Chicago · New York · San Francisco

Six Fairies on Vacation

One day, a long time ago, there was great excitement in Fairyland. All the different fairies were being put to the test: they had to find their way out of the Green Maze in the park. The first six to succeed were to win a holiday in Gnomeland as a prize.

That's how, one lovely day, Iris, the blue fairy, Apricot, the fat fairy, Pine Cone, the black fairy, Tulip, the red fairy, Nettle, the ugly fairy, and Orchid, the white fairy, left their home and set off for the Great Wood. "Be good!" came the Fairy Queen's gentle voice in the distance, "Be gooood!!" But the six fairies, excited at their new adventure, were out of earshot already.

Pine Cone went fastest, on her flying ladder, though she didn't fly at top speed, to avoid frightening the parrot. Iris, the blue fairy, had the most comfortable ride, in a magic armchair, while Apricot, the fat fairy, laden with food supplies, was the slowest, as she bumped along on her rolling pins. Orchid, the white fairy, dipped and soared on her chopping board. She liked to hover and admire the flowers. The wasps pulling Nettle's prickly carriage wanted to stop at the flowers too, but Nettle wouldn't allow that. She banged her peg leg with annoyance and firmly ordered them on.

"On you go!"

Tulip, the red fairy, cheerfully pedalled along on her sunflower tricycle, wondering what tricks she could play next.

"I'm dying to get there," she confided to Apricot, "Thank goodness, there won't be any Fairy Queen around always handing out good advice. And anyway, I'm bored with fairyland magic. What I need is to mix with ordinary folk for a while."

"Yes, indeed," agreed Apricot, paying not the least attention to Tulip. She was much too busy thinking about the gnomes' kitchen.

All the woodland folk and the gnomes were just as anxious to meet the fairies, as the fairies were to reach the wood. Everyone was bustling about, hard at work building six new houses. It was easy to scoop out the insides of the six giant gourds; the real problem was drying them out in time. A fire had to be lit in each, and in all the turmoil, Black Rat's whiskers were scorched.

"I wonder what they're like?" folk kept asking each other.

"They're bound to be very pretty," one of the Mouse Sisters said.
"And have lovely clothes," remarked another.
"Will they have a magic wand?" Mole was asked.

"Of course," he replied, "A magic wand, magic rings and magic potions. All fairy objects are magical."

Mole had but a single thought in his head: to get one of the fairies to make him a hole in the ground—a far, far deeper one than he himself could ever dig. He wanted to find out what there *was* deep down in the earth. There must be *something*, mustn't there?

So the gnomes hammered and drilled holes and painted. The Fairy Queen had already told the magician gnome about the visit, and he had said to the woodland folks:

"Things must be done properly. Their homes must be ready for them when they arrive. You'll soon find out what a lot can be learned from the fairies.

"Hurry, the fairies are coming."

It is an unforgettable experience. I met one once, when I was younger and my beard not so white. She made two of the fingers on my right hand vanish into thin air. I found them again, two days later, when I blew my nose!"

The Tournament

The fairies had been in the gnomes' village for two days. They had visited the wood and met all the inhabitants. Apricot had eaten traditional gnome dishes such as stuffed mushrooms and cheese, peas in honey brandy, strawberries, raspberries and blueberries with cream.

Now, the gnomes and the woodland folk were secretly preparing a really special event: a tournament.

A real jousting tournament, with mounts (tortoise-mounts of course), knights, banners, lances and prizes— the lot! And a huge grandstand was erected in the village square for the six guests of honor.

The square was covered with red clay and the lanes in which the knights were to fight marked with flour. In the meantime, behind the fence, the "knights" were getting ready. Redbeard the giant was certainly the favorite. For though the magician gnome's magic ring had shrunk him to gnome size long ago, he was still the

"Wait till you feel this, Redbeard."

strongest of them all, and strength is very important in a tournament. That's why Firebrand, the smith gnome, stealthily slipped a horse shoe into the padding on the end of his lance, muttering to himself: "This'll give that nasty Redbeard a crack!"

"Don't hurt each other!" implored the doctor gnome, as at Trumpeter Mouse's signal, the knights charged each other, and the contest began.

Firebrand and Redbeard were the first to bite the dust. Firebrand caught a blow under the chin, and he came back to his senses a few minutes later, asking what time it was. His own iron blow had landed on Redbeard's jaw. Not only was Redbeard bounced from the saddle, but he didn't touch solid food for a week, for he couldn't chew a thing!

However, the most incredible part was yet to come. Goopy, the clumsiest gnome, who was also nearsighted, didn't notice the pole with the crown of laurels for the winner in the middle of the field. He crashed right into it. His lance was knocked across his chest so that it caught the wrong opponent under the chin, sending him flying.

Goopy's own opponent was run down by another knight's mount that had swerved to avoid bumping into Snail— who had heard the starting signal but hadn't had time to get out of the way. This meant that the only knight still upright was Goopy, clinging to the pole. Everyone else had been more or less knocked to the ground. So Goopy was declared the winner. He was led to the grandstand, amid great applause and asked to remove his cap.

Suddenly he realized what was about to happen and he started to blush. In fact, he turned as red as a beet and, with everyone watching, Iris, the blue fairy, planted a big kiss on his forehead. Goopy was so embarrassed he slid off Tortoise's back, and Tortoise himself chuckled merrily. Then little Goopy was carried off, shoulder high.

"She kissed me! She kissed me!" he kept exclaiming, almost swooning with joy . . .

Nobody had ever thought that Goopy would win the tournament!

This was the prize . . .

The Magic Wand

Of all the fairy objects, it was the magic wand belonging to Iris, the blue fairy, that most aroused the curiosity of the gnomes and the woodland folk.

"I wonder what magic it can work?" someone remarked.

"I wish it were mine!" exclaimed someone else.

In the end, Bunny plucked up enough courage to ask Iris a certain question . . .

". . . Fox's brushy tail! That's what I'd like! Can you get it for me?"

"Certainly!" replied Iris, "As long as Fox is willing to exchange his tail for your tail!" Bunny hurried off in search of Fox, who had no objections. Iris's magic wand quickly did the trick. Bunny paraded about swishing his new tail, and Fox was quite relieved at having got rid of his bulky brush.

Suddenly, there was great confusion. Folk started clamoring to exchange bits of themselves: Hamster got Hare's long ears, Tortoise and Snail swapped shells, Frog and Badger exchanged coats. Then matters took a difficult turn when folk wanted something new without giving anything in return. Iris, however, granted every wish.

"I want to swim like a fish" said Otter, "but without becoming one!" With a flick of the magic wand, Otter found himself half–fish. Then it was Bear's turn. The greedy bear was so anxious to get his paws on honey that he decided to turn into a bee. One of the gnomes, who had forgotten how many centuries old he was, asked if he could become young again.

"Will that do?" Iris asked, as with a tap of her wand, the gnome found himself stroking a fine black beard.

"And this?" as Firebrand became a red-headed youngster again. In short, everyone made a wish and each wish came true.

Wild Piglet, who had always longed for a fine pair of tusks like his Grandad, found he had acquired the ivory tusks of an elephant.

Crow, willing to try anything to hide his bald patch, was delighted to hand over his hat in exchange for some of Hedgehog's prickles.

Grasshopper asked: "Could I have longer legs, please, so I can do high jumps?"

But when he got them, he found that the higher you jump, the harder the

"This is magic!"

landing, and he wound up with a great lump on his head.

The Twin Mice had a much more original idea: one was left-handed, so without telling his twin, he asked Iris to make him right-handed. Imagine his astonishment when he learned that his twin brother had asked the fairy to make *him* lefthanded!

Caterpillar put forward a request for roller skates, so he could move faster.

"Fairly small ones, Miss Fairy . . ." he said politely.

"Make us any color you want: yellow, green, blue or lilac, but not red, and no spots," said the Ladybirds.

"Tip tap! Tip tap!" Cricket did his little dance in front of the fairy. "I can't do special effects with only two feet!" he complained. And so he acquired a tiny beaver's tail so he could keep time with the music.

The ever-sensible Ants each asked for a large basket, though once they'd filled them they could hardly move.

Absolutely everyone wanted a change of some kind.

Then the trouble started. The gnomes and the woodland folk began to wish they could go back to things as they were before. It was Cricket who first put their thoughts into words.

"Whew!" he groaned, perspiring heavily, "this tail's too heavy!"

In a very short time, there was muttering and moaning about the magic, and the general grumbling soon swelled to a chorus of loud complaint. At last, the fairy called them around her and said, smilingly:

"Would you all like to become your old selves again?"

"YES! YES, PLEASE! Oh, yes . . ." they cried.

So with a tap of her magic wand, the fairy worked wonders again, and they all became their own familiar selves. There they stood, rubbing their eyes, amazed at their strange experience, but in their hearts, so glad that nothing had really changed. And as they drifted away, still talking excitedly about the day's events, Iris, the blue fairy, head a tiny voice. It was Caterpillar, struggling along, holding his roller skates.

"They're . . . they're . . . too fast for me!" he gasped.

"Learn to walk before you run!" said Iris.

"Perhaps it was better before."

Ice Cream

It was the end of May, and the air mild with summer just around the corner. The gnomes decided to dig up some of the ice they had buried during the winter. One of their ancestors, Zag, the magician gnome, had invented the system of burying ice in winter, when it's plentiful, and storing it for use in summer. When Apricot, the fat fairy, saw all that ice, her first thought was of ice cream.

"You must know what ice cream is?!" she exclaimed, "There's no such thing as summer without ice cream!"

As it happens, the only sweet delicacy known in the wood was the Bees' honey, and that was scarce and difficult to get, for the Bees hated parting with it. So when Apricot mentioned that ice cream was the most scrumptious of all goodies, folks' mouths began to water.

"I need flour, milk, eggs and heaps of sugar," Apricot said to the volunteer ice cream makers, "and don't forget

"Next one!"

chocolate and all kinds of fruit too!"

"Sugar? Chocolate?! What are they?" came a flood of questions.

"Oh, dear! I quite forgot you don't know! You don't have them! Well, find some chestnut meal and honey. I've a magic recipe that will do nicely," said Apricot, taking her recipe book from her pocket.

Then the fairies shooed everyone away, for like all cooks, Apricot was jealous of her own recipes and liked to keep them secret. In the meantime, all those who just *knew* that Apricot was going to produce a marvelous treat, skipped lunch; while those who didn't, were sorry that evening, when the skillful cook laid out her works of art.

For, together with the ice cream, there were cream cakes, almond cake and whipped cream—a real feast. Never before in the living memory of gnomes had such a spread been seen!

In days to come, the magician gnome kept taking off his cap and gazing dreamily into it, saying with a sigh, "What a lot of ice cream you hold!"

Somehow, nobody ever discovered exactly how, news of the ice cream traveled far and wide. People making trips to distant spots must have mentioned the feast, for the following summer, Crocus, the magician gnome, received a message from the North Pole. "The People of the Great Icy Wastes would like to ask you, our brothers in Warmer Lands, to help us make use of the ice, our only resource, and obtain ice cream. Please tell us how. Please reply soon. Signed: Willy Walrus."

By sheer bad luck, however, the magician gnome could do nothing to help, for by that time Apricot had returned to Fairyland, taking the secret of ice cream with her.

The Enchanted Mirror

Nettle's enchanted mirror was the talk of the village, and the woodland folks and gnomes were longing for the day when the sheet draped over it would at last be removed. But Nettle seemed to enjoy stirring their curiosity.

"The Mirror's sleeping, and the magic's turned off," she said. "I'll tell you when it wakens. Then you'll see the marvels it can work!"

Then one day, the fairy announced: "The enchanted mirror is awake, and it says it will double whatever is asked of it."

Everyone went wild with excitement. Fox was the first to push his way forward and, being conceited, he asked for a double tail. Then came Bear's turn and he got a twin brother to play with. Tortoise was granted another scooter, and so it went. Only Water Rat was unhappy when after staring fixedly into the Mirror he discovered he had grown two new pairs of eyes and ears.

Nettle grinned from behind the mirror. "Come along, have two of whatever you fancy. It's all free of charge. Just say thank you!"

"Thank you, dear fairy!" they echoed, as they were granted their wishes. The line of those waiting was never-ending . . . Then the fuss began. Stoat made a dreadful mess when he tried to pile eggs into his basket. Beaver discovered he couldn't play more than one trumpet at a time, so there was no point in having spares. Black Rat fell flat on his face, half-blinded by three pairs of spectacles all crammed on his nose at once. And Twin Bear was turning out to be a rather tiresome

"I have a surprise for you . . ."

brother for, after sharing the honey for a bit, the two Bears began a fist fight!

Worst of all were the Bumble Bees. They had all been given two extra pairs of wings. Now they could fly faster, but it took far too much effort to stay in the air! And, in the meanwhile, Nettle gloated and urged: "Come along then! There's plenty for everyone!"

Magpie, who loved jewelry, couldn't stop admiring herself in the Mirror. As she did so, she suddenly had a surprising idea: "I've heaps of jewelry already. Double strings of beads are ever so vulgar and I'm not the type to go about dripping with ornaments. What I'd like," she said, hopping up to the enchanted mirror, "is a double mirror! So, if one should get broken . . .

(though I hope that doesn't happen—it brings bad luck)". And before Nettle could raise a finger to stop her, she had propped her own little hand mirror in front of enchanted mirror. Instantly, there was a frightful crash and the enchanted mirror shattered into a thousand pieces.

Mirror against mirror: the one thing that should never be done! One of the two is always destroyed, and though the fairy mirror was bigger, it was the more fragile, and it broke. Not that this was really a terrible disaster in the end; for after the first flurry of excitement, the fun of having things doubled was beginning to wear off.

"Oh, well!" Nettle sighed to herself, "Just as I was beginning to enjoy myself! But I'll soon find another trick to play on them . . .!"

"Oh, how careless of me. I've broken the Enchanted Mirror," exclaimed Magpie.

The Concert

It was Orchid, the romantic fairy, who remembered that the Fairy Queen would have a birthday soon. Some silly person asked the Fairy Queen's age.

"That's a secret," the fairies replied. "It's one of the things we're not allowed to tell."

The magician gnome had been secretly in touch with the Fairy Castle through his crystal ball, and he would have a chat with the Fairy Queen from time to time. When he found out about her birthday, he began to think of a nice present for her.

He remembered he ought to have a broken crystal ball lying about. He found it after a long search and luckily got it back into working order. Then he polished an old jewel box. The Fairy Queen's birthday present was now ready.

Orchid was invited to deliver it, so she climbed onto her flying chopping board and silently sped away.

"What a lovely present!" said the Fairy Queen, "How kind of them! I must thank them all, woodland folk, gnomes and everyone. They really are very nice, especially their leader, the magician gnome. Crocus, isn't that his name?"

"Yes, your Majesty", said Orchid. "They are kind, and we're having a lovely vacation. They live quite a happy life in an unspoiled world, and they want you to be happy, too. Now, all together, we're preparing a surprise for your birthday evening. Please open this box on the stroke of midnight, and then listen. I can't tell you any more!"

With a polite curtsy to the Fairy Queen, Orchid rushed back to the wood for rehearsals. Yes, rehearsals! You see, it was a concert! A concert

Crocus kept in touch with the Fairy Queen . . .

with all kinds of instruments, and with the audience joining in at the opening chorus and at the end.

"One, two, three," the musicians stopped, "one two three," they held their breath, "one, two, three . . . ." Orchid flicked her baton and the notes of five violins rang out as one. The concert had begun.

The sound of such sweet music brought a tear to the eyes of the soft-hearted members of the audience. Then Redbeard's banging on the drums made them jump in their seats. With smart flicks of her baton, Orchid conducted the orchestra, and at each movement, one of the instruments rang out clear and loud over the others, in perfect harmony. What beautiful music! How clever they were! And if there was a stray voice out of tune—

well, the orchestra drowned out any little mistakes!

Back in her Castle, the Fairy Queen gazed into the crystal ball and listened, enthralled, to the music. Suddenly, she saw that the picture was blurred. As she wiped the crystal ball with her hand, she noticed it was damp.

"That can't be a tear!" she said in disbelief, "I can't cry! Fairies never cry!" She quickly pushed such a thought out of her head. And though she knew that no one could hear, she clapped delightedly at the end of the concert.

Suddenly, all over the musicians and the audience, fell a shower of sweets, flowers, cherries, beads, rings, whistles and pencils: something for everyone. The Fairy Queen had worked one of her wonders.

"What a lot of presents," said Frog to himself, in wonder.

23

Do to Others as You Would Have Them do to You

A cake-baking competition will be held on Sunday afternoon, in front of Dormouse's house, to decide the winner of the best cake in the wood. Entries invited. You may be the winner! Good luck! Have a good time!

Tulip

After the unforgettable day when Apricot had proved how clever she was at baking cakes and making ice cream, the woodland folk found they had a sweet tooth. What's more, the gnomes' trousers were now far too tight around the waist. Yes indeed! They had grown fat by stuffing themselves with cake.

One day, as they were all enjoying the "sweet delights" of the table, many of them received a strange letter, which read like this:

"A cake-baking competition will be held on Sunday afternoon, in front of Dormouse's house, to decide the winner of the best cake in the wood. Entries invited. *You* may be the winner! Good luck! Have a good time!" signed Tulip, the fairy.

Instantly, there was a frantic hunt for ingredients (especially honey), and before long, the Bees were forced to hang out a sign saying "No honey left." The great day dawned at last, and the table was set out for the occasion. Tulip watched the competitors arrive with their cakes. At the beginning, they were all very pleasant to each other.

"Did you put vanilla or cinnamon in your sponge cake?" one of the Mouse Sisters asked Tortoise.

"Neither. I used ground salt crystals," replied Tortoise, who had inherited a taste for salty food from her marine ancestors.

"What a huge cake!" they all said to the giant, though some muttered enviously: "Whopping, but empty! And probably inflated with air from his bellows!"

"Ha, ha, ha!"

As time passed, however, the remarks grew even less friendly, for each cook began to feel his or her's was the finest cake and deserved the prize.

In the meantime, Tulip was moving from cake to cake, tasting each—a finger dipped in the cream, a morsel here and a cherry there–exclaiming as she went:

"Very good!"

"Delicious!"

"Scrumptious!"

"Mmmm! Lovely!"

And though Tulip heaped compliments on each cook for fine baking, not a hint did she drop as to the likely winner. She just went along, nibbling a crumb here and munching a slice there.

Now, the other fairies, who had also entered the cake competition, were showing signs of irritation.

"Just wait!" grumbled one, "I bet Tulip has organized the whole show just so she can guzzle cake at our expense!"

By now everyone had exactly the same suspicion, as Tulip tripped along the cakes, still exclaiming with delight.

It was the giant that unwittingly brought matters to a head. Weary of watching the fairy demolish bits of cake, he grumbled: "If they're all so good, why not just give the prize for the biggest!" When Apricot heard the giant's words, she shrieked with fury, for she was certain none of the cakes was better than her own.

"Try this one before you speak!" she cried. And she threw her own lovely cake right into the giant's face.

This started the cake fight.

After patiently listening to Tulip's flattery over all their efforts, the cooks were all now very angry at not being awarded the prize. They simply picked up their entries, and in a flash, cakes went spinning the length of the table. There was quite a rumpus, and anyone seen roaring with laughter was generally silenced by a squishy cake in the face.

Tulip stood and watched the battle. Never before had she enjoyed so many delicious pieces of cake, and followed by entertainment, too! And all she had needed to do was write a handful of invitations!

"Ha! Ha!" she laughed, "you all wanted to win . . ." But she never ended the sentence. Someone facing her ducked to avoid a large cream cake, and the next thing Tulip knew, she was sitting on the grass. Her entire face, except for one eye, was a mass of sticky custard. Suddenly, she stopped enjoying herself.

"Do to others as you would have them do to you!"

"Splosh!"

A Slice of the Moon

Nobody knew that it was his diet that gave the black fairy's parrot his rainbow colored feathers.

"He can only eat petals," explained the black fairy, "but they must be colored, and I haven't any left. Would anyone care to help me pick some more flowers for the parrot?"

However, the woodland folk and their friends rather disliked the parrot, for he was a haughty bird. Perhaps because of his bright colors and the fact that his mistress was the black fairy, he looked down his beak at people. He also had a craze for repeating what he overheard, and nobody liked that. What's more, if you made rude noises at him, he made even worse ones back!

In spite of all this, one of the gnomes volunteered to pick flowers, and as he confided to a friend, there was a reason. "We can then ask the fairy for a favor, later. I suspect she could make me become the most famous gnome of all!" He then told his friend about a plan he had and some of the others quickly joined in. They picked petals until the delighted black fairy had plenty with which to make her parrot's food. And the Woodland folk and their friends patiently waited until she at last asked the question: "What can I do for you, after all your kindness?"

"Well . . . we don't know if it's possible . . . we *would* like . . . but we don't want to take advantage . . . if you could . . ."

"Speak up! What would you like? Don't worry, just ask! Nothing ever surprises a fairy! Anyway, I'm one of the oldest and nothing amazes me any longer! Now then!"

"Well, we'd like to go to . . . . to the moon!"

"Go to the moon?" said the fairy, "The moon! Now, that's never been done before by gnomes or woodland folk . . . well, I'll see what can be done!" The black fairy stood lost in thought, twisting the magic ring on her forefinger.

"There's a crescent moon in three days' time," she said at last, "so we'll

"Here's the food . . ."

place a ladder against that slice of it. A specially long ladder, just for you. All you'll have to do is climb up and down it. Off you go and get ready! There's no time to lose!"

Three days later, as night fell, there was such confusion at the foot of the ladder that the climbers had to elbow their way towards the rungs. The crowd watched them enviously: the lucky ones who'd soon be setting foot on the distant moon.

"If I'd known, I'd have gone petal-picking, too, for the parrot," the spectators murmured. But it was too late. And as the crowd cheered, the little group scrambled up the ladder.

The Bumble Bees went first. Off they flew and alighted on the rungs higher up for a rest. Soon all the little figures grew smaller and smaller as they vanished into the distance. Up they went, but the farther they climbed, the harder it became. They soon felt very tired, while the moon, standing still in the sky, seemed no nearer. The little group climbed for hours, but the moon was far, far away.

The Bumble Bees were the first to give up. They unpacked their parachutes and floated down, too weary to fly. By then the gnomes and their friends realized it was all a mistake. They would never have the strength to climb all the way to the end of the ladder. They would have to go back. The return journey, however, was a nightmare, for when they peeped over their shoulders, they felt dizzy and shook with fright. In the end, they all set foot safely on the earth.

Pine Cone, the black fairy, was waiting for them.

"Poor things!" she said soothingly, "you must be worn out! Here! I picked up your clogs when they fell off as you were going up!" She hugged Bear, the weariest of all, and gently pushed him towards the table.

"These are the slices that are best!" They're yellow like the moon, but much closer to home!"

"These slices of melon will cheer you up. They look just like half-moons."

The Ring's Revenge

Tulip, the red fairy, loved playing practical jokes. One day, she saw the magician gnome leave home with his mushroom basket over his arm. Suddenly, she had a great desire to peep into the Great Book of the Gnomes. However, she found it no easy matter to get through the magician gnome's back window, and as she squeezed through, she said to herself:

"Help! I'm growing smaller and smaller . . ."

"It's just as well I'm not fat like Apricot!"

Inside lay flasks, magic potion tubes, the crystal ball, strange pieces of apparatus, horns, dried flowers, strange bags of colored powders and, there, on a large wooden stand, the Great Book itself, bound in leather.

Her heart thumping, for she knew this was forbidden, Tulip turned over the yellowing pages of the ancient book. Now, during her stay in the land of the gnomes, Tulip had learned to read some of the peculiar gnome writing. The secrets of the Great Book of the Gnomes were about to be revealed. Between the pages describing the spell of the Magic Ring, she came upon the Ring itself. However, she carelessly pushed it aside and went on leafing through the Book.

Now, with her long nose and tiny eyes, the red fairy was no beauty, but she was incredibly vain. And when she

reached the chapter on "Beauty and Spells For Looking Attractive," she drank in every word.

"This is just what I require!" she said to herself, carefully copying the ancient spell. "I would never have believed the gnomes had such a knowledge of beauty treatments," she told herself. Then a thought struck her. "Why haven't they ever used them? They badly need improving themselves! Anyway, that's their business!" and she wrote down the following words:

"If your nose is too long, soak it seven times in a deep cup, on seven consecutive days at the stroke of midnight, counting up to thirteen, using this mixture: 33 thimblefuls of Royal Jelly from a healthy Queen Bee; add drops of verbena extract and slowly mix, adding a teaspoonful of violet juice each time you stir. Leave for three days and nights in a copper bowl. Take 100 ants' eggs, some snail's milk, a pinch of sulphur, a fair amount of belladonna blossoms and bluebell pollen. Grind the ingredients finely with a pestle. Add them to the mixture in the copper bowl, and use. This will shorten your nose."

"Good!" she exclaimed, "Now I'll have a prettier nose than Iris has!"

Where was she to get the Royal Jelly?

"Of course!" she said, clapping her hand against her forehead, "the Magic Ring! It'll make me tiny enough to slip into the hive!"

Picking up the Ring, the fairy quickly turned to page 777 and found the spell. However, just as she was shrinking so swiftly that the Great Book seemed the size of a house, the Ring slipped from her fingers. Scurrying under the door,

she ran into the garden. The flowers and leaves were now a thick forest, she was so small. It's so difficult trying to make your way through, when you're so tiny! She had a feeling that everything around her was growing strangely bigger and bigger.

"What is happening?" she wondered, "That daisy stem looked much shorter a moment ago!" Then it dawned on her! *She* was shrinking faster and faster . . . the Magic Ring was indeed casting a spell on her—but she did not know how to stop it!

Later, when the magician gnome went home with his mushrooms, he saw the Ring lying on the floor, near the Great Book. "I could have sworn I'd left it inside" he said to himself, puzzled. "Well, if somebody does sneak a look inside the Book, he won't know that spells have to be read backwards. Anyone reading a spell as it's written will fall under the Terrible Non-Stop Shrinking Curse!"

"Look! There's the Ring!"

King of the Deep

Since the day Magpie smashed Nettle's enchanted mirror into a thousand pieces, the fairy had been hunting everywhere for a new sheet of glass. Actually, fairy mirrors are not glass at all; they're made of a rare ice, found only in pure, crystal-clear waters. That's why, when winter came, Nettle began to wander far and wide, searching for a pool of sparkling water.

She strayed so far that one day she reached the North Pole. Her wooden leg creaked as she crunched over the frozen surfaces. Then, as she stared down through the thin film of top ice, Nettle could see, far below, each tiny detail of the bed of the sea. And she knew her search was over. She stooped to carry away a piece of the wonderful ice, when a distant glitter caught her eye. Five huge gorgeous pearls lay gleaming on the bottom of the sea.

Nettle's heart began to beat faster. Not even the Fairy Queen herself owned such splendid pearls. The thought of a dip in the middle of winter didn't appeal to her very much, but she was tempted. There the pearls lay, gleaming and shining even more clearly than before. Nettle could not help herself: she took a very deep breath and dived in. The ice cold water chilled her to the bone, but there were the pearls, almost within her grasp. Indeed, not only pearls awaited the fairy, but necklaces, gems, precious jars, rings and crowns too. There in front of her eyes was the richest treasure trove that ever a fairy could wish for. Nettle forgot all about the cold. She caressed the jewels, held them up and tried them on. Oddly enough, the single deep breath she

had taken was enough to last her all that time. Suddenly, she realized her clothes had gone, and that her wooden leg had vanished, together with her good leg. She now had a long silvery tail.

"Great Fairy! What has happened to me?" She saw her reflection in the pearly surface of a shell. How different she had become! So much prettier, with long dark hair and almond eyes. Never in her life had she heard of such a change in a fairy! Motionless, a pair of sea horses lazily gazed at her.

"Welcome!" boomed a deep voice, suddenly.

A very strange person was coming towards her, half-man, half-fish, swishing his large tail. There—his flowing white hair swaying in the water, a coral crown on his head—was the King of the Deep.

"So you're fond of jewels, are you?" he remarked, "Here, you may have as many as you desire: pearls, diamonds, silver and gold . . . if you remain here."

" . . . remain here? — Nettle replied —

But I don't want to! I *do* like jewels, but not enough to give up my freedom. So . . ."

"Ah, no, my dear!" exclaimed the King, in menacing tones, "You are no different from the other maidens. You all want the Giant Pearls, but without having to stay behind and keep me company! Here, you'll be a queen, with a throne of mother-of-pearl. The finest fish will be your footmen. You ought to be proud of the honor I do you!"

Poor Nettle felt a dart of fear at the thought that she, a fairy, so familiar with magic, had fallen under a spell. But when she thought she need never have to drag a wooden leg any more, she became more cheerful.

"Queen of the Deep? Yes, that might be better than just being a plain fairy." Nettle began to lay her plans.

"And in time, I might even win him around to my way of thinking . . . In the meantime, I'll soon make him forget about luring down other maidens. Then, as time goes by . . ."

"These jewels will be yours, my dear, if you stay and keep me company."

The Nightingale

In the days that followed Tulip's disappearance, the woodland folk spent all their time searching for her. She had not gone back to the Fairy Queen, and no one had any idea where she might be.

Only the magician gnome was seized with a terrible doubt: "I wonder if . . . . . No! She couldn't . . . ." he told himself.

And like the others, he tried to forget her mysterious disappearance, till only Orchid continued to wander in the woods calling her lost friend.

Orchid, the fragile, delicate fairy, that loved music, poetry and all beautiful things, missed Tulip even more than the others did, though the two had quite different characters.

One day, where the birch wood gives way to a forest of old firs, Orchid stopped to listen to the sweetest nightingale's song she had ever heard.

She knelt in amazement. How could such a little bird sing such wonderful notes, without the slightest mistake? "It really is a nightingale!" she said to herself.

This nightingale, however, was different from the others. The fairy sat entranced, listening to its song, then decided she would like to see the bird. But the instant she drew near to the fir trees, the bird abruptly stopped

"What a lovely song. I wonder where it's coming from?"

singing. And in the silence that followed, the wood seemed to disapprove of the fairy.

Orchid often visited the same spot, but each time, she was able to listen to the song only from the birch wood, and the moment she went closer, the bird stopped singing.

The fairy was soon obsessed by the nightingale's song. She longed to hear it from close by, as though to make it her very own. But she did not know how to succeed.

Then she remembered she could work her fairy magic and have her wish come true.

She began to concentrate and, with a deep sigh, she turned into a little chickadee. Still near the birch wood, she easily fluttered into the high branches.

From her perch there, she could hear from which direction the song was coming. She flitted from bush to bush, through the fir wood to where the light barely filtered down through the tall trees.

Nearer and nearer to the song she flew. Her fairy heart, now that of a little bird, beat with excitement.

How she longed to sing in chorus with such a gifted friend! But now she was very close to the nightingale, almost within sight of it — there, beyond that pine tree!

All that divided her from the voice she was anxious to reach was a thorn bush. She flew into its branches. She alighted on a dead twig and stretched her tiny body through the thorns to see across a beam of light.

"There he is!" she told herself, opening her beak to trill a greeting. But as she did so, one of the thorns, so feared by all the woodland creatures for their poison, pierced her breast.

Two of the gnomes saw the little chickadee next day, lying beside the thorn bush. A tiny drop of blood stained her breast, her little eyes closed forever.

The gnomes never knew what had happened. They dug a grave for the little bird and placed some flowers over it.

But only the woodland folks that lived in the neighborhood noticed that, from then on a nightingale always perched on the thorn bush to sing his song.

Another amazing thing happened, too. Not long after, one by one, all the thorns dropped off the bush and . . . A miracle! On the leafless bush, a host of brightly colored flowers suddenly blossomed in their place!

. . . the bush burst into flower . . .

A Fairy's Heart

None of the gnomes or the woodland folk had ever remarked on which of the six fairies was the best. But Iris would be the one they would miss the most when she left. She was nice to everyone, never giving herself airs about being a FIRST CLASS fairy. Yes, you see, fairies are divided into three classes. Only the very superior fairies, with special merits, are given First Class status by the Fairy Queen.

After the episode of the magic wand, which had caused so much excitement, the wand seemed to have disappeared. It was as though Iris had hidden it deliberately.

She had become very friendly with the Mouse Sisters and often went to their house for tea and a chat. However, all the woodland folk and their friends were struck by her amiable graciousness, which meant that they all went to her for advice, help or just to enjoy her nice manner.

The only person who never went anywhere near her, and indeed seemed to avoid her, was Goopy. The fact was, he only *seemed* to avoid her; because since the day he won the Tournament and got a kiss from Iris as a reward, he was always hanging about in the distance. Sighing deeply, he would spy

on her when he thought no one was watching. And Crocus, the magician gnome, shook his head every time he met Goopy, for he knew that the poor gnome had fallen in love.

"It's puppy love!" he said to himself. "Goopy'll get over it. He's young still. Ah! I was just the same at his age! . . . At any rate, he did get a nice kiss!"

Time passed in the wood, with the usual routine train of events. Then one chill November night, when the new moon was in its first quarter, Iris was in the wood. Now, each fairy had her own booster star or planet. Once a year, on a day known only to the fairies, she drew a new supply of energy from it. And tonight Iris had to gaze up at the moon. She stood without moving for hours on end, staring at the moon's pale crescent; then after repeating a spell, she started to make her way out of the wood.

"Brr! It's freezing!" she said to herself, as her feet sank into the snow. "If I'd stayed much longer, I'd have frozen to death!"

As she passed the knotted roots of an old fir tree, she looked for a tiny light she had noticed as she entered the wood. It came from the Crickets' cot- tage. Peeping in, she saw the flicker of a dying candle. Then, as she bent closer to peer at the Crickets, she real- ized that their tiny stove, supposed to keep them warm all winter, had gone out.

"Oh, dear!" sighed Iris, "they'll die of cold! They'll catch pneumonia in this icy weather, even under those thick blankets!"

The Crickets' home was very small, and Iris had to bend double to see her little friends. Instinctively, she breath- ed over them, and her warm breath soon filled the cottage. Iris knew that this was the only way to keep them alive throughout the night. If she left them while she went for help, they would be dead before her return. So, kneeling in the snow, she breathed steadily into the little house. Dawn finally came, but too late for the little blonde fairy, as she grew weaker and weaker. When the sun rose over the white wood, the little fairy was an ice-clad figure. One of the gnomes chanced upon her later and gave the alarm. The Crickets had been saved, but the kind-hearted fairy would never again delight the woodland folk with her sweet smile.

When dawn came, she was a statue of ice . . .

The Good Deed Machine

It seemed a morning just like any other, but this was to be a day to remember in the history of the gnomes. But to begin at the beginning. First of all, Queen Bee buzzed up in a rage, with a band of Fighter Bees. She swept straight over to the magician gnome, and the two started to argue. Then off she flew, slamming the door and shrieking: "No more honey till the culprit's been found!"

A little later, the magician gnome appeared in the doorway, scowling, and barked an order: "I want all the gnomes to assemble in the village square in an hour's time!"

Clearly something had happened! But how serious it was became clear when Crocus began: "Not only do our laws forbid stealing and punish thieves, but absolutely never, ever, since I've been King of the Gnomes, has a gnome committed such a crime. Queen Bee has just told me that one of you stole her Royal Jelly in the night! And the thief was very lucky that the guards were too sleepy to catch him! But I have proof it was one of you, for he left a gnome's clog-print behind! Now who was it? The culprit must confess and take his punishment!"

In the silence that fell, nobody moved a muscle.

"I want to know who is the thief!" thundered the magician gnome, "and

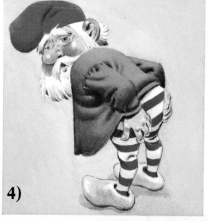

1) The Queen Bee complained

2) The Magician Gnome decided to punish the culprit

3) The culprit went into hiding

4) Poor Dandelion was punished, though he was innocent

if he doesn't own up, then you'll all be punished!"

Still nobody moved. The woodland folk, looking on, felt quite alarmed. Then at last a gnome stepped forward.

"I did it!" he said, gazing at Crocus, "Punish me!"

So the gnome was seized, trussed up and put onto the spanking machine. And never before had it worked so hard.

Then the meeting ended. Justice had been done! However, the matter was not to end there.

Two gnomes setting off to cut broom in the long grass, noticed one of their comrades skulking there. When they caught up with him, they saw his face was swollen to twice its size.

"What happened?" they asked him. The poor gnome replied tearfully: "It was the Fighter Bees!"

The spanking machine had punished the wrong gnome! This, of course, was put right when the real thief was given his ration of spankings. But what about the innocent victim? The gnome who had saved his friends from punishment? Who was going to make amends for his unfair spanking? All the others, and especially Crocus, felt dreadfully guilty about it all.

Apricot, however, found a way of putting things right. She brought the unfortunate gnome, still rather sore after his spanking, a glass of blue elixir: fairy nectar.

Apricot, the Fairy Queen's favorite cook, was the only one who knew the secret of this wonderful elixir that only fairies could obtain.

By now, everyone was quite envious of the brave gnome, and the fairy topped the occasion by outlining a marvelous plan to the magician gnome.

The gnomes were to build a machine that would be the judge of good deeds and award a prize to the best. Anyone feeling he deserved a reward would have his deeds justly analyzed by this good deed machine.

"I must leave you now," said Apricot. "The Fairy Queen wants me to come back to the Castle. I hate to go, but I must obey."

Crocus, with his crystal ball, tried in vain to persuade the Fairy Queen to let Apricot stay with them a little longer, but only Pine Cone, the black fairy, because she was so old, was allowed to stay.

"I've retired from work," she told Crocus.

So Apricot greased her rolling pins and left, while the woodland folk, the gnomes and the giant waved goodbye.

And the last to say goodbye was the black fairy's parrot, which kept on croaking:
"Say hello to the Fairy Queen! Say hello to the Fairy Queen!"

Titles in this series

Meet the Woodland Folk

The Woodland Folk Meet the Gnomes

The Woodland Folk Meet the Giants

The Woodland Folk in Fairyland

The Woodland Folk Meet the Elves

The Woodland Folk in Dragonland